THE GIFT of the INUKSUK

BY MIKE ULMER *and* ILLUSTRATED BY MELANIE ROSE

Sleeping Bear Press
310 North Main Street, Suite 300
Chelsea, MI 48118
www.sleepingbearpress.com

© 2004 Thomson Gale, a part of the Thomson Corporation.

Thomson, Star Logo and Sleeping Bear Press are trademarks
and Gale is a registered trademark used herein under license.

Printed and bound in Canada.

10 9 8 7 6 5 4 3 2 1

Library of Congress Cataloging-in-Publication Data

Ulmer, Michael, 1959-
The gift of the Inuksuk / written by Michael Ulmer ; illustrated by Melanie Rose.
p. cm.
Summary: Many lives ago, a young girl in what would become the Nunavut
territory of Canada builds stone men, called Inuksuk, to direct her father and
brother home when they are lost in a storm while hunting caribou.
ISBN 1-58536-214-X
1. Inuit—Juvenile fiction. [1. Inuit—Fiction. 2. Statues—Fiction. 3. Nunavut—Fiction.
4. Canada—History—Fiction.] I. Rose, Melanie, ill. II. Title.
PZ7.U3485Gi 2004
[Fic]—dc22   2004005955

To Cecelia Ulmer,
WHO KNOWS HOW TO SURVIVE IN THE WILDERNESS.

Mike

For my best friend, Terry.

Melanie

The flag of the Canadian territory of Nunavut bears an Inuksuk as its symbol. Once seen only in the North, groups of Inuksuk, known as Inuksuit, look down from roadside perches across Canada.

In gardens and campsites and trailheads across North America and even around the world, Inuksuit bear a message from the land and those who have come before: you are not alone.

A few stones can form a greeting, a guidepost, or warning. They can mark a tragedy or the scene of a great event. Inuksuit require no money, no electricity, not even a common spoken language. All that is needed is a builder, a few stones, and the knowledge needed to decipher the Inuksuk's message.

The Inuit knew animals captured in the hunt were not game so much as allies, willing to sacrifice their lives so the Inuit could

continue theirs. That's why the bear whose rib supplied a hunting knife was often depicted on the knife's handle.

Because obtaining the staples of life was never easy, the Inuit harvested only what was needed and used every bit of what they took. Connected to the earth, they used her gifts wisely and reverently.

It is that spirit of connectedness that makes traditional Inuit life a model for civilizations around the world and makes the Inuksuk such a worthy symbol for all.

The Gift of the Inuksuk is not an Inuit legend. Those stories belong to the Inuit people to tell. Still, it's my hope a little girl I have called Ukaliq can represent the wisdom that made the Inuit rich partners in the bounty that is the natural world.

—Mike Ulmer

Many lives ago, an Inuit girl dashed through a land of snow and stones and caribou and stars. She was small and inquisitive and always, always running. Her father said she reminded him of the Arctic hare, the *ukaliq*. From that day, she was known as Ukaliq.

Ukaliq loved to be outside where she could juggle and wrestle with her brothers and sisters. Her feet would barely touch the thin grass that cloaked the earth in summer or winter's blanket of snow.

Ukaliq learned to gather cotton grass for the wicks of her lamps. Her mother showed her how to use bird bones for fine needles and the teeth of the caribou for ornaments on clothing.

There was water from which to fish, snow from which to build homes, animals, large and small, bears and seals, and most important of all, the caribou, to provide all the Inuit people would need.

Ukaliq and her family were grateful, to the Creator for the bounty of the land, to the whale who brought blubber for food and oil for light, to the caribou and the seals and the bear who gave of themselves so the Inuit could live.

Everywhere Ukaliq looked, she saw gifts. Even the hardest ground would grudgingly provide stones and wherever Ukaliq's family lived, the little girl would stack the stones into friends.

Some of Ukaliq's stone friends looked ready to shout of joyous things. Some seemed filled with sorrow. Some pointed past the horizon or toward a lake. Through the long nights of winter or the endless days of summer, Ukaliq's stone people rose, like sentinels, from the earth that had cradled them.

When the caribou have short hair, they are ready for their migration to the south. As they did every year, Ukaliq's father and brothers embarked on the hunt.

They were only gone a day before a great storm drained the colour from the earth.

She missed her father and brothers and longed for their safe return. But Ukaliq also understood the importance of the caribou. A great hunt meant ample food through the snowy season when there is little game. It meant skins for warm clothing and new tents. Caribou bones could be used through the winter to scoop out the snow. Their tendons were made into thread for delicate embroidery.

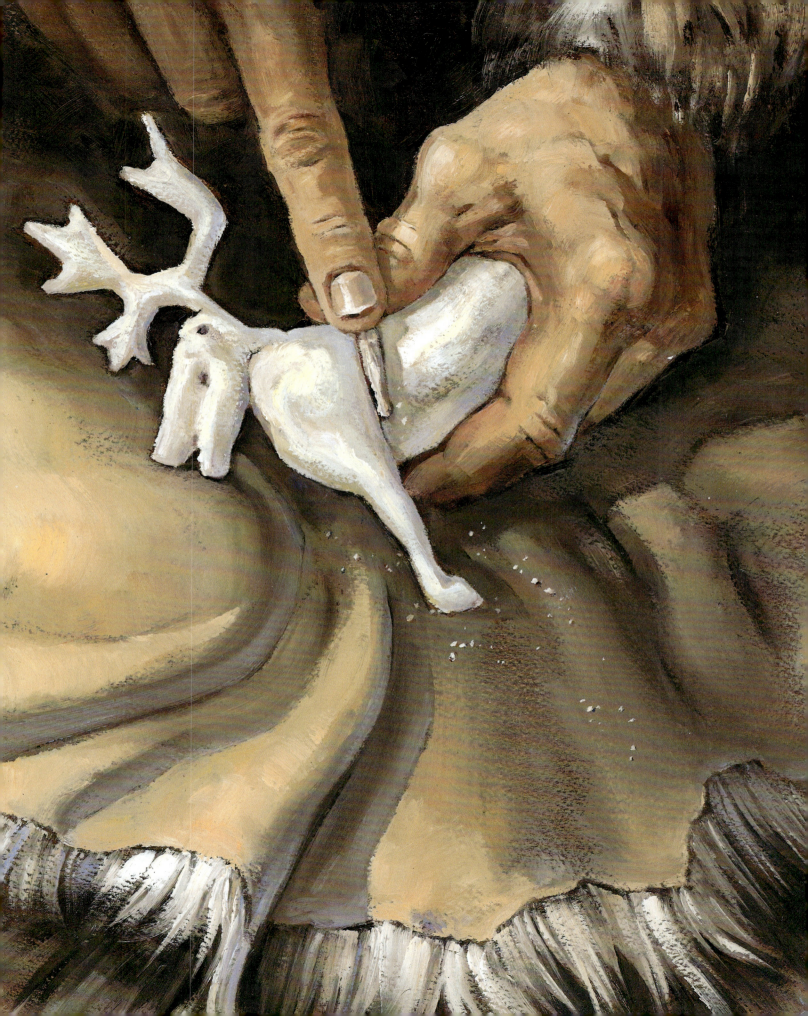

Every morning Ukaliq would wake hoping to see her father and brothers but instead her eyes would fall only on her piles of stones. If only, she thought, she could use her stone friends to bring her father and brothers home safely. That's when Ukaliq realized what she should do.

She called together her younger brother and sisters. "Remember the stone people I have built?" she said. "They will help return our brothers and father."

Ukaliq and her brother and sisters shifted one stone man only as far as could be seen through the snow from another. Ukaliq showed the children how to put sticks inside the figures to create arms to point toward home.

The next morning she heard a voice. "Ukaliq,
your friends showed me the way home."

Before she could speak, she heard someone
shout, "Come quickly!" The stone figures had
done more than guide the men home.

They had brought the caribou.

Ukaliq waved her arms and directed her younger
brother and sisters. When the caribou dashed for an
opening between the stone figures, Ukaliq would head
them off but Ukaliq knew the caribou were wise and giving.
The caribou understood that like the stones pulled from
the earth that had guided them or the fish speared from
the rivers, they played a part in the life of the Inuit.

The hunt was the best in memory. The night was festive and filled with laughter. The winter passed with many throatsongs happily shared among the women.

Soon a name was given for Ukaliq's stone people:
Inuksuk, or, *in the image of man*. Inuksuit was a
gathering of more than one Inuksuk.

Ukaliq would grow from a girl to a woman and
each year, more of her Inuksuit would, like a moss
on a great stone, spread across the North. Some
would be used to indicate a dangerous passage.
Others pointed travellers toward home.

Different kinds of Inuksuit were used to direct the eye to a distant place and to denote where there had been great hunts. Songs describing Inuksuit were composed by elders and passed on to travellers. That way, the traveller could find his way to his destination by remembering the song.

To this day Inuksuit wait for paddlers and canoeists beside shallow lakes. They greet travellers along great highways. They carry a message an Inuit girl shared with her father and brothers, a message between man and animal, between place and people... here within the bounty of the Creator, you are not alone.

MIKE ULMER

Mike Ulmer keeps an Inuksuk at home but he does not need it to find good fishing. The Inuksuk reminds Mike of the way the Inuit People of the North live a simple life and consume only what they need.

Mike lives in Hamilton, Ontario, Canada with his wife Agnes Bongers and their three daughters: Sadie, Hannah, and Madalyn. When he is not learning about Inuksuit, Mike writes a sports column for the *Toronto Sun* newspaper. Among Mike's books are *M is for Maple: A Canadian Alphabet* and *H is for Horse: An Equestrian Alphabet.*

MELANIE ROSE

Melanie Rose lives in Mississauga, Canada with her son Liam, and their two cats, Mickey and Meesha. Melanie teamed up with Mike previously on *M is for Maple: A Canadian Alphabet.* She has also illustrated *Z is for Zamboni: A Hockey Alphabet, K is for Kick: A Soccer Alphabet,* and *H is for Homerun: A Baseball Alphabet.* She is a graduate of the Ontario College of Art.